today i am

Wendy Sutton

NEWMAN SPRINGS PUBLISHING
320 Broad Street
Red Bank, NJ 07701

First originally published by Newman Springs Publishing 2021

ISBN 978-1-63881-006-3 (Paperback)
ISBN 978-1-63881-007-0 (Digital)

Printed in the United States of America

For my girls, with all my love

Today I am...

Today I am a lion. I run, I chase, I roar.

Today I am a seagull that dips,
and twists, and soars.

Today I am a ladybug. I crawl, I tickle, I fly.

Today I am a flower, bending
when winds pass by.

Today I am a shark. I swim, I eat, I dive.

Today I am a honeybee working in my hive.

Today I am kitty. I meow, I lick, I sleep.

Today I am a whale that glides into the deep.

Today I am an elephant. I bathe, I sun, I blow!

Today I am a turtle that's really, really slow.

Today I am a cheetah. I hunt, I climb, I run.

Today I am an alligator soaking up the sun.

Today I became so many different things!

Now let's just wait and see...
All the things I will be tomorrow
when imagination carries me!

about the author

Wendy is a wife and mother to two teenage daughters. She lives in East Texas with her family, including one exceptionally fantastic dog named Sally. She's real good at formulating thoughts, but putting those thoughts into spoken words doesn't always come easy. Poetry has been an outlet for Wendy. It's something that has allowed her to speak when spoken words may fail and something that has voiced her heart when it's probably best to hold her tongue. When her girls were little, Wendy often read to them before bedtime. *Today I Am* was inspired by those nights. Those wonderful, sweet, cherished nights when sleepy eyes would close and dreams would begin. Wendy hopes that through her work, you find those same moments with the ones you hold dear to your heart.

CPSIA information can be obtained
at www.ICGtesting.com
Printed in the USA
BVHW091216231121
622347BV00017B/813